BUNNY ROO
and
DUCKLING TOO

By Melissa Marr

illustrated by Teagan White

Nancy Paulsen Books

to Kaden, my wee chaos.
Love, Mama -M.M.

to Luna & Shanley -T.W.

One day you woke...

and hopped out of bed.
I thought you'd
become a frog,

so I brought you
to the pond.

When you touched the water,
you squawked and splashed.
I thought you'd
become a duckling,

so I jumped in
to play with you.

When you saw me, you climbed
on my back and chattered.
I thought you'd
become a monkey,

so I took you
to the trees.

When you saw the forest,
you squirmed and twisted.
I thought you'd
become a snake,

so I slithered
next to you.

When you saw the
wide-open fields,
you raced so fast.
I thought you'd
become a cheetah,

so I ran with you
to the garden.

When you saw
the rows of carrots,
you sniffed and nibbled.
I thought you'd
become my bunny roo,

so I fed you
a heaping salad.

Then you
snuggled closer,
and I knew.

You are my everything,
as fun as all the
animals in the world.

NANCY PAULSEN BOOKS
An imprint of Penguin Random House LLC, New York

Nancy Paulsen Books is a trademark of Penguin Random House LLC.

Visit us online at penguinrandomhouse.com

Library of Congress Cataloging-in-Publication Data
Names: Marr, Melissa, author. | White, Teagan, illustrator.
Title: Bunny roo and duckling too / Melissa Marr; illustrated by Teagan White.
Description: New York: Nancy Paulsen Books, [2021] | Summary: A mother demonstrates how much she loves her child
by pretending to be various animals her little one reminds her of as they share a busy day.
Identifiers: LCCN 2019053894 | ISBN 9780525516040 (hardcover) | ISBN 9780525516057 (ebook) | ISBN 9780525516071 (ebook)
Subjects: CYAC: Mother and child—Fiction. | Animals—Infancy—Fiction.
Classification: LCC PZ7.M34788 Bs 2021 | DDC [E]—dc23
LC record available at https://lccn.loc.gov/2019053894

Manufactured in China by RR Donnelley Asia Printing Solutions Ltd.
ISBN 9780525516040
1 3 5 7 9 10 8 6 4 2

Title and text hand-lettered by Teagan White.
The illustrations were done in watercolor and gouache.